BIZARRE BUGS

goldenrod aphids

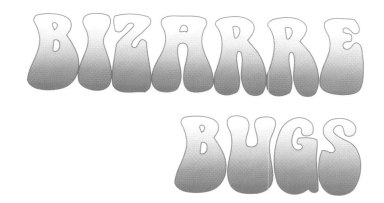

BIZARRE BUGS

By Doug Wechsler

Photographs by the Author

COBBLEHILL BOOKS/Dutton

New York

FOR SADIE,

the world's best sowbug catcher

ACKNOWLEDGMENTS

The Author would like to thank the following people for their helpful comments and suggestions: Charlie Alovisetti, Lois B. O'Brien, Daniel Otte, Tracy Pedersen, and Kyra Wiens.

Library of Congress Cataloging-in-Publication Data

Wechsler, Doug
    Bizarre bugs / text and photographs by Doug Wechsler.
        p.   cm.
    Includes index.
    ISBN 0-525-65181-0
    1. Insects— Juvenile literature. 2. Animal defenses—Juvenile
    literature. [1. Insects. 2. Animal defenses.] I. Title.
    QL467.2.W38 1995
    595.7–dc20   94-27432   CIP   AC

Published in the United States by Cobblehill Books,
an affiliate of Dutton Children's Books,
a division of Penguin Books USA Inc.,
375 Hudson Street, New York, New York 10014

Designed by Charlotte Staub
Printed in Hong Kong   First Edition
10 9 8 7 6 5 4 3 2 1

Why Be
Bizarre?

Insects have some pretty odd shapes. If you think about it, even common insects are strange compared to other animals we know. A fly is like a huge pair of eye clusters on wings. A butterfly is a slender bug trapped between two gigantic, painted sails. A firefly, or lightning bug, is a creature with a chemistry set tacked on behind.

Many insects are even stranger. Some wear long streamers of wax, faces like alligators, or fancy polka dots. What would cause some insects to be so peculiar?

Every one of these unusual features has a purpose. Each has come about to help the insect survive. A feature that helps an animal to survive is called an **adaptation**. An adaptation allows an animal to adjust to its environment. For example, wings allow insects to escape enemies. They also allow them to travel to food sources or to find mates.

Insects were already common 300 million years ago, well before the age of dinosaurs. Since the first insect appeared, **evolution** (ev oh LOO shun) has caused numerous adaptations in insects. Evolution is the change of plants and animals into new forms. When an insect evolves a useful adaptation it is more likely to survive and reproduce.

New adaptations have helped insects to survive and branch out into so many different species. Nobody knows how many kinds of insects exist. At least one million, and possibly as many as 30 million species, live on earth. Let's look at some insects with bizarre adaptations and see why these adaptations have evolved.

The Strangest Bug of All

What is the strangest insect you can think of? The peanut-head bug is probably even stranger than that. The name, peanuthead or alligatorhead, already tells us a lot about an odd **planthopper** from the rain forests of Central and South America. Indeed, the head looks much like a peanut or a smiling alligator. Not only does the peanuthead bug look bizarre, it also acts in some bizarre ways.

Though it is called a bug, it is not a true bug. Scientists use that name only for members of one group of insects. Later, we will meet a few true bugs, such as the stinkbug and ambush bug. Many people use the nickname, bugs, for all insects.

The peanuthead bug has many adaptations to help it escape its enemies. Though they are big — eight centimeters long (over three inches) — they are hard to see. At a distance they look just like the whitish bark of the trees they live on. A close look at what looks like an eerie grin on the head of the peanuthead bug may be enough to scare away a few enemies of this harmless creature. If this doesn't work, it will fly off and land with its wings open. Suddenly the enemies is faced with eyespots that look like a huge pair of eyes. *Eeeek!* The eyespots are bigger than the eyes of the **predator** (an animal that eats other animals).

But, why such a big head? The head actually contains a sac. The sac stores tree sap that the peanuthead bug sucks up through its strawlike mouth. So you see, camouflage,

A peanuthead bug on tree trunk

2

A peanuthead bug flashing eyespots

bizarre looks, and flashing eyespots are actually useful adaptations. They help the peanuthead bug escape or feed. Let's take a look at how other adaptations help insects escape their enemies, communicate, and survive.

Mantis camouflaged on bark in Philippine rain forest

Avoiding the Enemy

Many insects avoid their enemies by hiding. Still, not everyone can hide. There are only so many crevices, rolled up leaves, and spaces beneath stones. Often these hide-aways are already taken. Others have hungry spiders, sala-manders, or other predators lurking within. There is another way to hide. It's called **camouflage**.

Camouflage means a disguise that hides. Most insects are camouflaged by having colors and shapes that blend into their backgrounds. Bark-colored mantises rest on bark. Green caterpillars hide on leaves. Grouse locusts are grasshoppers that often specialize in hiding on rocks. Their coloration makes them hard to tell from the rest of their habitat.

Camouflage may go one step further. Walkingsticks and many species of inchworms look and act like sticks. Caterpillars may resemble the vein of a leaf. Treehoppers line up on a branch and look exactly like thorns. If we had to give out a blue ribbon (or better yet, a green and brown one), it would go to the katydids.

Katydids are the kings of camouflage. Katydids are rela-tives of grasshoppers. They are common in tropical forests.

Walkingstick in Pennsylvania

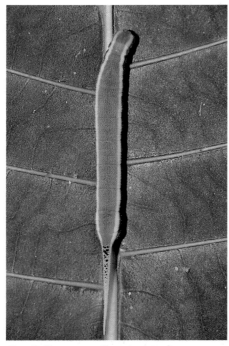

Caterpillar camouflaged on leaf vein in Costa Rica

At night they walk about on leaves and stems. There are thousands of species of katydids and they come in an amazing variety of shapes, sizes, and patterns. Many katydids look exactly like leaves. Leaves in the jungle are usually marked by insect damage or have lichens (LIKE enz) growing on them. So it is with katydids. Often they look like leaves with lichens or with holes chewed in them. During the day katydids sit still out in the open, hidden by their clever disguise. A hungry, insect-loving monkey in the tree-tops might leap right past them. Only under cover of darkness are katydids free to walk about.

Camouflage is also important to predators. For example, a tiger's stripes help it avoid dangerous people and ambush prey. Like the tiger's stripes, the camouflage of some insects not only protects them, but also tricks their prey as well.

Dead leaf-mimic katydid in Ecuador

Ambush bug on goldenrod flower

True to its name, an ambush bug hides quietly among goldenrod flowers. It is waiting to strike its prey with its oversized front legs. It eats insects such as flies, butterflies, and small bees which use their good eyesight to seek out flowers. When a hungry fly lands on the flower for a meal, it finds itself the dinner rather than the diner. It would have noticed the ambush bug if it hadn't blended in so well with the yellow flowers.

It Pays to Advertise

While many insects hide by looking like something they are not, others tell the world, "Look, I am here!" A bad-tasting, poisonous insect does not want to be confused with a

Bright colors of toxic grasshoppers warn predators

good-tasting one. It could be halfway down a frog's mouth before the frog realizes the mistake.

Poisonous insects often show off with bright colors. The colors warn their hungry enemies, "Don't bother to bite me, you wouldn't like it." Multicolored grasshoppers are generally poisonous. The bright colors warn birds and other animals not to eat them. The bright orange of familiar insects such as ladybugs and monarchs are also warning colors. These insects are poisonous to birds, people, and many other animals.

Where do insects get their poison from? Many get it from the plants they eat. Plants have many chemicals to keep insects from eating them. But, for almost every poison plants have, some insect has evolved a way to survive it.

Milkweed is a common wildflower with a poisonous white sap. The poison can cause heart failure in many animals. Caterpillars of the monarch butterfly and a number of other insects munch on milkweed. The monarch keeps the poisons in its body even after it has become a butterfly.

Monarch butterflies and their caterpillars, milkweed leaf beetles, milkweed bugs, milkweed longhorn beetles, and milkweed tussock moth caterpillars all eat milkweed. All sport bright black and yellow or orange colors.

Experiments have been done with blue jays and monarch butterflies. If the blue jay has never eaten a monarch before it will try it. But it will quickly spit it back up. Once it has tasted a couple of monarchs it will never again try to eat one.

Monarch caterpillar

Fakes and Bluffers

Some insects with warning colors are fakes. They mimic or imitate a more dangerous species. The viceroy butterfly is one of the best known. It looks almost exactly like a monarch. It is sometimes edible, but you can be sure that a blue jay will not try it.

The frangipani (franj eh PAN ee) sphinx moth caterpillar wears the same black, red, and yellow of the poisonous coral snake. This fat caterpillar might make a nice meal, but many predators are afraid to attack. Some animals may be born with a fear of this color pattern. It looks too much like a deadly snake.

Frangipani sphinx moth caterpillar

Viceroy

Leaf-mimic katydid in Peru

Same katydid displaying bright colors

For one kind of katydid from the Amazon Basin, camouflage is not enough. As we have seen, a lot of katydids look just like dead leaves. But this well-camouflaged katydid has a second line of defense. When a bird sees through its disguise, it attacks the katydid. Plop, the katydid drops to the forest floor and spreads its wings. Surprise! Suddenly the bird sees only the flash of bright colors on the back side of the insect's wings. The bright colors somehow confuse the bird. The katydid no longer looks like something good to eat. If the bird hops to the other side, the katydid will turn so that its bright underwings still face the attacker.

Dirty Business

Brown lacewing **larvae** (young ones) don't throw their trash away. In a way, you could say they recycle it. Little hooks on their backs hold onto the rubbish. In fact, these

10

Trash-carrier   *Leaf beetle larva protected by its own droppings*

larvae are called trash-carriers. Soon they become covered with the remains of their prey. Uneaten pieces of the insects they have eaten completely conceal the trash-carriers. This is the perfect defense — who wants to eat garbage to get the bug? It is a bit of a shock to see a little junk heap suddenly walk. Only the tiny legs give the hoax away.

Larvae of certain leaf beetles never drop their droppings. Instead the droppings form clusters curling over the tops of the insects. The larvae become completely hidden beneath the arch of poop. They sure don't have to worry about anything eating them!

Hairs, Spines, and Prickly Tines

All insects wear their skeletons on the outside. Instead of bones they have an outer covering called the **exoskeleton** (ex oh SKELL eh ton). The exoskeleton is made up of different layers. Inside it is tough and flexible. The insect's muscles attach here. The middle layer is often hard and stiff, except at the joints. It forms the armor. On the outside is a very thin layer which is waxy. This is the insect's raincoat. It keeps water from getting in. At the same time it

11

Caterpillar hair foils attack of army ants

keeps the insect's gooey insides from drying out. Exoskeletons take on many forms, they can be hard or soft, smooth or wrinkled, horny or hairy.

What good is hair? A caterpillar's furry coat can form a shield against the jaws of ants. If they try to get close enough to bite they get poked in the face. Hair also makes insects unpleasant to swallow. Most birds avoid hairy caterpillars.

Hairy caterpillars may look cuddly, but they are not always fun to pet. Some, like the woolly bear, are quite harmless. Others may have hairs coated with stinging chemicals. Just touching one of these exotic caterpillars lightly may cause a painful sting.

Other caterpillars are armed with spines. The Io moth caterpillar may not look dangerous, but beware. It will leave you with a painful rash. Spines of caterpillars some-

Tropical Io moth caterpillar

Spiny katydid, Panacanthus

times act like the doctor's shot. Touching the spine causes it to shoot poison. The poison works much like the sting of a hornet and is just as painful. No wonder so many spiny caterpillars sport such bright colors. The colors cry out a serious warning. Don't touch me...or else!

Certain grasshoppers and walkingsticks also present a thorny problem to would-be predators. These insects are covered with spines. In fact, one South American katydid is so covered with prickly spines it has earned the scientific name *Panacanthus.* That means "all thorn" in Greek. Their thorns will draw blood from the tongue of a hungry frog or the fingers of a curious scientist. A swift kick with a spike-covered hind leg may discourage all but the boldest enemies.

Phony Targets

Insects have a number of adaptations to foil the aim of their attackers. Among the most common are phony targets. False eyes are one example. Many butterflies and other insects have small eyespots on the rears of the hind wings. These serve a different purpose than the large eyespots of the peanuthead bug. A bird thinks it is aiming for an eye to

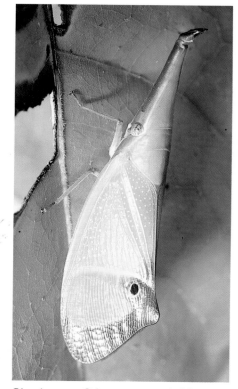

Planthopper Odontoptera *with false eye on the end of its wing*

kill the insect. Instead, it harmlessly hits an eyespot. The prey doesn't lose its head — only a bit of wing.

Some planthoppers have another kind of phony target. They produce long streamers of wax from their backsides. Nobody knows exactly what these are for, but scientists have a few good ideas. The long, waxy streamers may serve as targets for birds. A bird that eats flying insects, such as a **jacamar**, might snap first at the wax because it is a more obvious target. The wax just falls off and the bug flies to safety. Eventually though, some birds learn the trick and grab the other end.

Young planthoppers may have so much wax it's hard to

Planthopper with waxy streamers

Jacamar with same species of planthopper

14

Planthopper nymphs with wax in Borneo

tell that they are insects. They often grow up together in large groups and form a fluffy cluster. What bird would attack a tangle of wax? A wax blob just doesn't look like food.

Tympana on katydid's legs

Sometimes it seems insects were left with the spare parts in nature's tool kit. We expect ears to be on the head, noses to do the smelling, and jaws to do the chewing. This is not so with insects. Evolution has led down many paths. Insects use different tools to hear, smell, eat, and do other things we all need to do.

Leg Ears. Can You Hear With Your Legs?

Male katydids spend much of their time singing to find mates. In fact, it's their song that gives them their name. They "sing" by vibrating their wings rapidly. This causes the edges of the wings to scrape each other. One edge has teeth like a comb or saw. The other is smooth like a violin bow. Try running your fingernail up and down the teeth of a comb and you will know how they make their music. Some species seem to sing the word "katydid" all evening.

Katydids have no ears on their heads, but they can hear. Just how do the female katydids hear the love songs? Katydids have a slit on each leg covered with a thin membrane. This leg ear is called a **tympanum** (TIM pan um). This membrane works like our eardrum. When sound waves hit it, it vibrates. The vibration sends waves through a hollow space in the leg. Hairlike cells in this space trigger nerves. The nerves carry signals to the katydid's brain telling the female whether she is listening to her own species.

Many moths also have a tympanum, but most don't use it to listen to other moths. They are listening for the high pitch squeaks of bats. Bats are their mortal enemies. Bats can locate moths, branches, and cave walls with the echoes of their squeaks. This is called **echolocation** (EH ko low CAY shun). When these moths hear a bat they fly in a spiral or drop to the ground as if dead.

A few moths in the woolly bear family use the bats' sensitive hearing against them. These moths can make noises. The noises mix with the echoes of bats to confuse the bats while the moths make their getaway.

Most other insects have no tympanum, but some can sense sound with tiny hairs on their body or antennae. The hairs vibrate with the sound waves in the air. They don't hear clearly in the way we do, but one message usually gets across. Danger!

Antennae

What do martians and moths have in common? They both have antennae. The bushy antennae of male moths give them an alien look, but they are not an adaptation to scare anyone. Instead, they work more like television antennae. Rather than radio waves, they pick up chemical signals called **pheromones** (FEHR ah mones).

Pheromones are chemicals made by one animal that send a message to another animal of the same species. In this case the message to the male moth is "come here." The male moth uses his antennae to follow an invisible chemical trail to the female. His antennae are extremely sensitive.

Male luna moth antenna

Each antenna may have over a million microscopic holes for the pheromones to enter. Inside the hole, the chemical causes a nerve to send a signal to the brain. It lets the moth know it is flying in the right direction.

While moths' antennae look like feathers, antennae of katydids look like hairs. Often they are very long — up to four times the length of their bodies. Among other things, the long antennae of katydids in tropical forests help them

Katydid crouching and freezing — note super long antennae

Midge

to sense the flight of bats. Movement of the air causes the katydid to crouch and freeze. Holding themselves close to the branch, they appear like a part of the branch to the bat's sonar.

Bats do not only hunt katydids by echolocation. They also hunt them by listening for the songs of males. Bats are numerous in tropical forests. For this reason it is too dangerous for jungle katydids to sing endlessly like they do in North America. Instead, they sing short quick songs. They also vibrate their bodies to send messages to other katydids on the same bush. While vibrating, they wave their long antennae in circles around their bodies to sense hungry spiders that might also feel the message.

Antennae have many uses aside from being long-range noses and enemy detectors. Antennae of ants and many other insects can also "taste" objects they touch. In this way they act much like our tongue. The feathery antennae of male midges (a fly relative) and mosquitoes can hear and locate females. Other insects' antennae act as moisture detectors or as thermometers to sense changes in temperatures.

Ferocious Jaws

Can you imagine being the size of a fly and facing the jaws of a stag beetle? The jaws of the male stag beetle are almost as long as its body. Each forms a mean-looking hook. Maybe being so tiny wouldn't be as bad as it seems. Stag beetles feed on sap, not other animals. Sap is the liquid from the stems of plants — the blood of plants. A stag beetle saves its tremendous jaws for battle with its own kind. The males joust with their awesome jaws.

Now look up at the mouth of an army ant major (soldier) from South America. Its jaws are only four millimeters (1/6 inch) long. But they are one-third the length of the whole

Stag beetle

ant. She (majors and workers are all females) uses these chompers to defend other members of her colony. Her jaws can grip like a tiny bulldog. Still, a bite in the finger is not that painful. It's the rear end of the ant you have to watch out for. As it bites with its jaws, it stings like a small bee. *Yoweeee!*

Monster jaws are not much good for working. The smaller jaws of the army ant major's little sisters are better tools. They are made for cutting much like scissors. With them the worker ants grab escaping insects, tear their prey apart, and carry the pieces back to the colony headquarters.

Army ant major jaws

No Jaws, Just Straws

The opposite of the monster jaws of the army ant major must be the beak of a stinkbug. Most stinkbugs use their skinny beaks to suck the juices of plants. Some stinkbugs also prey on other insects. Tiny barbs on the beak keep the prey from getting off. It will then suck the juices out of the live insect with its strawlike mouth.

If all you ever ate were milk shakes, you would survive quite well with a mouth like a straw. Butterflies and moths survive on only liquid foods. Many sip nectar, the sugary water made by flowers to attract insects. But, did you know that some moths and butterflies drink sweat, minerals in wet soil, turtle mucus, sap, and other liquids?

Stinkbug feeding on leaf beetle

"88" butterfly licking author's pants to dissolve salts

Butterflies have ways to drink some solids as well. Imagine you are a "strawmouth" and there is a pile of sugar on your plate. You also have a glass of water. What do you do? Butterflies have solved this problem. They can use their saliva to dissolve dried sugars or minerals then sip them up.

Seventeen-year cicada adults congregating on tree trunks in Ohio

Chapter FOUR

Bizarre Life Cycles

While some insects have odd looks or peculiar body parts, many also have bizarre life cycles. If you can think of an unusual way to live, an insect has probably come up with the idea before you.

It is not as though the normal cycles of insects are not strange enough. Most insects follow one of three basic life plans.

Silverfish and a few other primitive insects hatch out of the egg looking like tiny adults. They simply grow larger, **molting** (shedding their exoskeleton) each time they outgrow it.

Dragonflies, grasshoppers, cicadas, and others hatch into **nymphs**. During their last molt the wings develop and the nymphs become adults. In grasshoppers and many true bugs adults look just like nymphs with wings. In other cases the change can be dramatic. Dragonflies, mayflies, and stone flies start life as underwater nymphs looking nothing like adults.

The third plan includes one more major change. In butterflies, ants, beetles, and others life starts out when the egg hatches into a **larva**. Caterpillars, grubs, and maggots are

Cicada expanding wings as nymph transforms into adult

all examples of larvae. When fully grown the larva sheds its exoskeleton to become a **pupa**. In many cases the larva spins a cocoon of silk surrounding itself before shedding. The pupa is a resting stage. The pupa does not eat and barely moves at all. Unseen, inside the pupa, the wings develop and other changes take place. Finally an adult, totally unlike the larva or pupa, emerges. After expanding its wings and hardening its exoskeleton it usually flies off in search of food or a mate.

Invasion from Inner Space

Underground in the eastern United States lives an army of strange-looking beasts. Their big, hooked, hairy claws make them look like miniature monsters. The huge front legs are for digging. Beneath the surface they sink their tube-shaped mouths into roots. They sip sap slowly. In seventeen years they grow only two and a half centimeters (one inch). These are the seventeen-year cicadas.

Once, every seventeen years, the entire army of cicada nymphs creeps slowly out of the soil. Each leaves behind a round hole. Soon the ground looks like Swiss cheese. Each nymph crawls in slow motion to the nearest tree. Resting on the tree, its back splits open. The ugly creature inside leans back through the slit, freeing itself from the old exoskeleton. Over the next hour the insect takes on the more familiar form of an adult cicada. In a few days thousands of cicadas sing an earsplitting chorus.

Seventeen years old is ancient for an insect. Most insects live for less than one year. The seventeen-year cicada is among the record holders here.

Another Numbers Game

While cicadas live long, aphids die young. Aphids are tiny

26

Milkweed aphids

insects shorter than a pencil eraser. Like cicadas, they drink plant juices.

Most aphids hatch out of eggs in the spring. In a few weeks they grow to be adults. But these adults don't lay eggs. They give birth to live young. Strangely, the tiny aphids are born with baby aphids already starting to form inside. In a few weeks the new babies will be born. The new aphids will also be pregnant.

By the end of the summer there are millions of aphids. Only then do the aphids mate and lay eggs. The eggs survive the winter because they have an antifreeze-like chemical. The eggs hatch in spring and the cycle starts again.

Restless Wanderers

Nature has plenty of other cycles. The lives of army ants follow another type of cycle.

Army ants live in large groups — sometimes half a million ants. That is as many ants as there are people in a medium-sized city. Army ants feed on other insects. If they did not move around, they would quickly eat up all the food in their neighborhood. So, the ants must move the colony often.

Fortunately, army ants do not have to build a nest. They just hide in a hollow log or brush pile. They cling to each other foot to foot and form a football-sized cluster. The cluster is called a **bivouac** (BIV ah wack).

After dawn, ants swarm out of the bivouac by the thou-

Army ants on raid in Peru

sands. The ground becomes peppered with ants moving away from the bivouac in search of food. Soon the swarm of ants is only connected to the bivouac by a narrow trail. This trail is marked by a pheromone from the rear ends of the ants that used the trail.

At dusk ants at the swarm start forming a new bivouac. Under cover of darkness the whole colony crowds down a narrow trail of solid ants to the new bivouac. The workers carry the larvae in their jaws.

The colony of army ants moves like this nearly every night for two weeks. At the end of the second week it finds a hollow tree and moves in. There the larvae spin cocoons, shed their skins, and become pupae (PEW pea). The colony keeps its home base in the tree for three weeks, sending out raiding parties most days. During this time the queen lays 200,000 or so eggs.

The hatching of the cocoons signals that it is time to move. By now the eggs have also hatched and the cycle begins again — two more weeks on the road to terrorize the insect world.

Looks Ordinary, Acts Strange

Army ant swarms and professional football games have much in common. Both form big crowds. Football players are not the only ones making a living at the game. Army ants are not the only critters making their living at the swarm. Hot dog vendors, radio announcers, and even pickpockets profit from football crowds. Certain birds, insects, and mites could not survive without the swarm of army ants. Let's take a look at a couple of the crowd followers.

A tachinid (tack IN id) fly does not look all that different from a housefly. It's not satisfied with breeding in garbage like many flies we know. Instead, it spends its time hovering over army ant swarms. As the ants chase grasshoppers

Tachinid fly ready to lay egg on katydid being attacked by army ant

and crickets out of the leaves, the fly lands on them. It lays its egg on the grasshopper. If the grasshopper escapes the dangers of the ant swarm, it will die a slow death. A maggot will grow inside and later hatch out as a fly.

A number of butterflies also accompany army ants. But, why? To answer this we must first look at the birds. Several species of antbirds and woodcreepers follow the ants and feed on the fleeing insects. At one time there may be as many as twenty or more birds at the swarm. This means a wealth of bird droppings. Nothing goes to waste in the jungle. Some kinds of butterflies fly back and forth over and behind the ants looking for what the birds left behind. The minerals in the droppings are to the butterflies what vitamins are to you.

Why Are There So Many Kinds of Bugs?

As you see there are about as many insect life-styles as there are types of insects. If they all had the same life-style most, if not all, would soon die out. Think of what would happen if all insects ate one type of plant, or if all lived under the eaves of houses, or if all tried to camouflage themselves in the same way. They would run out of food and shelter and all would soon be eaten. Instead, the varied life-styles of insects allow so many species to survive together. Sometimes it pays to be different.

Glossary

Adaptation — A feature that helps an animal survive. Some examples are: a longer wing for faster flight, songs that attract mates, or special colors that give warnings.

Bivouac — A cluster of army ants. A bivouac is the army ants' nest. They form it by hooking their feet together. It is usually hidden in a hollow log or other shelter.

Camouflage — A pattern that hides an animal in its environment.

Echolocation — Sensing the world by hearing echoes. Bats hear the echoes of sounds they make. They can tell the shapes of things in their path. This includes insects they eat.

Evolution — The change of plants and animals into new forms. Over a long time animals may evolve new adaptations. They may also evolve into two or more species.

Exoskeleton — The outer covering of an insect. It is a tough covering. It protects the soft insides of an insect. Like our skeleton, it is where muscles attach.

Jacamar — A tropical bird from Central and South America. Jacamars have long thin bills. They are experts at catching flying insects.

Larva — The second stage in insects that have four life stages. These stages are egg, larva, pupa, and adult. Caterpillars, beetle grubs, and maggots (fly larvae) are all larvae.

Lichen — A fungus and an alga (one-celled plant) that live together. The fungus cannot live without the alga. Lichens often grow on tree bark.

Midge — A relative of flies that looks much like a mosquito. Some midges bite, some don't.

Nymph — The second stage in insects which have three life stages. These stages are egg, nymph, and adult. The young of dragonflies, true bugs, and grasshoppers are all called nymphs.

Pheromone — A chemical made by one animal that sends a signal to another animal of the same kind.

Planthopper — A large group of jumping insects. Most species feed on sap. Unlike most insects, the antenna is below the eye.

Predator — An animal that eats other animals.

Pupa — The resting stage between larva and adult in insects with four life stages.

Tympanum — The ear of katydids, crickets, and some moths. A tympanum is made of a membrane over a hollow space with hairlike cells inside.

Index